# BAMBOO

*For my mother, Gum-may, who knew China and farmed its land. - P.Y.*

*Published in 2005 in Canada by*
TRADEWIND BOOKS LIMITED
*www.tradewindbooks.com*

*Text copyright © 2005 by Paul Yee*
*Illustrations copyright © 2005 by Shaoli Wang*
*Book design by Jacqueline Wang*

*First Edition*
*10 9 8 7 6 5 4 3 2 1*

*Printed in Korea*

Library and Archives Canada Cataloguing in Publication

Yee, Paul
Bamboo / by Paul Yee ; illustrated by Shaoli Wang.

ISBN 1-896580-82-3

1. Chinese--Folklore--Juvenile literature. 2. Picture
books for children.
I. Wang, Shaoli, 1961-  II. Title.

PS8597.E3B35 2005    j398.8'089'951    C2005-902340-6

*The publisher thanks the Canada Council for the Arts and the British Columbia Arts Council for their support.*

Canada Council **Conseil des Arts**
for the Arts **du Canada**

BRITISH
COLUMBIA
ARTS COUNCIL
Supported by the Province of British Columbia

*Cataloguing-in-Publication Data for this book*
*is available from The British Library.*

# BAMBOO

By Paul Yee          Illustrated by Shaoli Wang

VANCOUVER   LONDON

One day, Bamboo, a young farmer, took
two baskets of beans to sell at the market.
There, peasants from far and wide traded
fresh fruit and greens, farm animals and
the latest news.

Amidst the noise and heat, Bamboo was enchanted by one girl's beautiful smile. He thought about her all the way home.

Bamboo told his older brother, Banyan, about the cheerful farm girl, Ming.

"She will make a good wife and bring our family luck," Bamboo said.

Banyan encouraged Bamboo, but Banyan's wife, Jin, disliked Ming from the day they met. Nevertheless, the two families agreed on marriage plans for Bamboo and Ming.

At the wedding, Ming presented Bamboo with a special gift.

"Bamboo seedlings!" her new husband exclaimed.

"Yes, we'll plant them and watch them spring to life and fill the sky."

By morning, new shoots were nudging up, and by the next day the stalks were tall and thick. In no time at all, a bamboo grove flourished.

At breakfast Jin complained, "I hate getting up at dawn."

"When the rooster crows," Ming answered, "the air blows fresh and cool. It's the best time of all."

"She's right," agreed Banyan and Bamboo.

After working in the field all day, Jin grumbled, "Farm life is such a burden. My back hurts, and my hands and feet are cracked. No wonder the townspeople laugh at us."

"Yes," Ming agreed, "the work is hard and the townspeople scorn us. But they feast on the food we grow and can't live without us."

Again the two brothers agreed with her.

When Jin gave birth to a son, Bamboo decided to go to the New World to earn money to buy more land for their growing family.

"You are wise and will do well," Ming said to him. "Come home safely."

"I'll return soon," Bamboo promised. "You're my greatest joy."

As soon as Bamboo left, Jin said to Banyan, "We must divide the fields."

"But this is family land, and it belongs to all of us."

"Bamboo will return a rich man," Jin mocked. "Worry about your wife and son."

So Banyan and Jin took the best fields, along with the plough and the buffalo.

Ming was only given the bamboo patch, an old water-wheel and a hut to live in. She had no tools to work the land.

But Ming wasn't worried. She cut some bamboo poles to till the soil. To her amazement, they jumped to life and began to plough the earth into neat furrows ready for planting, with no help from any human hand.

At the end of the day Jin smirked, "So, how much land did you till today?"

"I'm almost finished," Ming said.

Filled with curiosity, Jin decided to find out how Ming got so much work done in a day.

The next morning Jin secretly watched Ming at work in her field. When she saw the bamboo tilling the soil, Jin thought, *Those bamboo poles are magic! I must have them for myself.*

That evening Jin crept into Ming's field and tried to steal the magic bamboo. But the poles leapt up and beat her.

"Yow! Yow! Yow!" she yelped.

Jin ran home to her husband and wailed, "Sister-in-law used her bamboo poles to beat me! You must destroy them!"

"Leave Ming alone!" Banyan protested.

"Do as I say," Jin hissed, "or I'll tell the whole village you're a coward who refuses to protect his wife."

Under the moonlight, Banyan gathered up the bamboo poles, threw them into the river and watched the swift waters carry them away.

The next morning Ming couldn't find her bamboo poles anywhere. She cut down a new pole to carry the water buckets to the creek.

*It will take days to irrigate this field*, she thought, as she pedalled the creaky old water-wheel.

To her surprise, water began to flow up through the bamboo pole onto the higher land. Soon all her work was done.

From her hiding place, Jin saw everything and was furious.

When Jin got home, she smeared charcoal on her face and hands to look like bruises.

"Sister-in-law beat me with another bamboo pole!" she wailed to Banyan. "Look at all these bruises! This time make sure you destroy the entire grove of bamboo!"

"I told you to leave Ming alone!" Banyan exclaimed.

"Do as I say," Jin hissed, "or I'll tell the whole village you're a coward who refuses to protect his wife."

With a heavy heart, Banyan went to Ming's land, cut down all the bamboo and threw it into the river.

But Ming worked hard and readied her paddy for planting. Her heart rejoiced when the rice grew tall and strong.

One day a letter arrived.

*Dearest wife,*

*I have wonderful news. By Heaven's grace, I struck it rich with a lucky find of gold and will return on the next ship.*

*Your loving husband,*
*Bamboo*

Two months passed, then three, then four.

Ming harvested her crops, and the bamboo grove grew back. But her husband did not return.

Ming worried.

Early one morning a runner dashed into the village and called for Ming.

"I bring bad news," he said. "Your husband's ship sank at sea."

Ming was sad, but she refused to weep. In her heart she knew that Bamboo would return just as he had promised.

Every evening Ming went to the dock to wait for Bamboo.

And every evening the villagers brought her food. "Eat," they said. "Keep up your strength."

One evening, Jin followed Ming to the dock. "Your dinner smells wonderful," Jin exclaimed, helping herself to the food the villagers had brought. She ate so greedily that she didn't see her son fall into the river. Ming saw the splash, dove in and saved him. But a strong current swept her away.

Ming floated downstream until a pair of hands reached into the river and pulled her ashore.

"Ming, I've come back," sang out a familiar voice.

There was Bamboo, alive and well. Ming hugged him tightly.

"They told me your ship sank at sea."

"Yes, many lives were lost. I almost drowned, weighed down by a sack of gold on my back. But after I cut it loose, I rose to the surface and found myself surrounded by thick bamboo poles. I grabbed one and floated along with my shipmates. Soon a passing ship rescued us. Look, I brought the poles back."

"They came from our farm. Your brother cut them down and sent them to you."

The next morning Ming and Bamboo returned to their village. When Jin saw them, she fell to her knees and begged for mercy.

"Sister-in-law, I was wrong. I made your life painful, yet you saved my little boy. I was nasty, but you were kind. Please forgive me," she cried.

"Of course I do," said Ming, warmly embracing her.

When people from the nearby villages heard about Ming's bamboo and how many lives it had saved, they came to see the magical crop.

"This will make the best ladders!" exclaimed the carpenters.

"This will make the best scaffolding," said the builders.

"This will make the best carrying-poles!" cried the porters.

"We'll pay you well!" they all shouted.

Bamboo and Ming shared their good fortune with Banyan and Jin. And as their bamboo grove flourished, so did their family.

GOVERNOR-GENERAL'S LITERARY AWARDS
French: Illustration

1989 Poulin, Stephane

Benjamin & la saga des Oreillers

# . BENJAMIN .
## &
### LA SAGA DES OREILLERS

# .BENJAMIN.

### &
### LA SAGA DES OREILLERS

STEPHANE POULIN

ANNICK PRESS LTD., TORONTO, CANADA

Annick Press Ltd.
Tous droits réservés

Conception: Stéphane Poulin

Annick Press Ltd tient à remercier le
Conseil des Arts du Canada et
le Conseil des Arts de l'Ontario de leur aide.

**Données de catalogage avant publication (Canada)**

Poulin, Stéphane
    Benjamin et la saga des oreillers

Publié aussi en anglais sous le titre: Benjamin
and the pillow saga.
ISBN 1-55037-075-8 (rel.) ISBN 1-55037-074-X (br.)

I. Titre.

PS8581.0846B46 1989      jC843′.54      C89-094179-3
PZ23.P684Be    1989

Distributeur au Canada et aux Etats-Unis:
Firefly Books Ltd.
250 Sparks Avenue
Willowdale, Ontario
M2H 2S4

Imprimé au Canada par D.W. Friesen and Sons Ltd.

À Pierre Pratt,
dont l'amitié m'est si précieuse.

Benjamin était un petit-gros-monsieur-tranquille. Il était de nature plutôt timide et parlait peu. Par contre, Benjamin turlutait tout le temps et les gens disaient gentiment de lui qu'il ressemblait à un oiseau, bien qu'il fût beaucoup plus gros...

Benjamin habitait à la ville avec ses parents. Son père et sa mère restaient à la maison parce qu'ils ne travaillaient plus. Pour passer le temps, sa mère soignait ses cactus et jouait du tuba. Son père élevait des souris blanches et jouait de la harpe. Le soir, ils jouaient de la musique tous ensemble dans la salle de bain.

- Le son y est meilleur! disait son père.

- Dis plutôt que c'est parce que tu crains que nos voisins n'entendent tes fausses notes, ajoutait sa mère en riant.

Le matin, Benjamin embrassait ses parents qu'il aimait beaucoup puis partait travailler. Comme la plupart des gens de son quartier, il était à l'emploi de la manufacture d'oreillers.

Benjamin avait pour tâche de refermer par une délicate broderie
les oreillers bourrés de plumes. Cependant, on disait partout dans
la ville que ces oreillers n'étaient pas que de simples oreillers de plumes.
On disait de ces oreillers qu'ils étaient extraordinaires, et ce qui était
encore plus extraordinaire, c'est qu'on ne savait même pas pourquoi...

- C'est à cause des plumes d'oies! disaient certains.

- C'est à cause de ce que mangent les oies! disaient d'autres.

- Les oies sont ensorcelées! disait-on aussi.

- C'est peut-être tout simplement des plumes de sorcières!...

Tout ce qu'on savait à propos de ces oreillers extraordinaires c'est qu'ils procuraient un sommeil délicieux et profond. Un sommeil si profond que même les chatouillements d'une plume d'oie ensorcelée n'auraient pu interrompre. Grâce à de tels oreillers les gens pouvaient enfin dormir sur leurs deux oreilles. Même les veilleurs de nuit pouvaient dormir tranquille puisqu'il n'était plus nécessaire de surveiller les voleurs qui ronflaient de plus belle depuis que le sommeil était devenu si précieux.

La rumeur courut jusqu'aux villes voisines et bien plus loin encore. Enfin, un jour elle revint dans la ville sous la forme d'un petit autobus essoufflé, rempli de gens étranges. Les passagers qui en descendirent étaient de toutes les couleurs. On n'avait jamais vu ça. . .

On se doutait bien qu'ils venaient tous à cause des oreillers extraordinaires, mais encore?

- Ils viennent faire enquête, dit l'épicière.

- Ils veulent notre secret, pensa un client.

- Comment peuvent-ils voler un secret que nous ne connaissons même pas nous-même! ajouta un autre client.

En fait, tous ces gens venus des quatres coins du monde désiraient tout simplement acheter des oreillers pour les revendre dans leur propre pays.

Monsieur Arthur, le patron de la manufacture, leur fit visiter les lieux. Les visiteurs furent si enchantés qu'ils commandèrent des oreillers par milliers. Cependant, une dame, restée à l'écart, observait Benjamin qui turlutait.

- Pardonnez-moi monsieur, dit-elle en s'approchant de Benjamin qui leva les yeux et lui sourit. Comme il était de nature plutôt timide et qu'il parlait peu, Benjamin se remit à turluter.

- Mon nom est Mona DeLopera et je serais heureuse si vous acceptiez de venir turluter dans mon opéra, en Italie! Benjamin leva de nouveau les yeux et lui adressa un second sourire. Et comme il était de nature plutôt timide et qu'il parlait peu, Benjamin lui répondit tout simplement "oui!" et se remit à turluter.

C'est ainsi que Benjamin et ses parents partirent un jour pour l'Italie.

On ne parlait plus que des oreillers extraordinaires et du succès international du trio familial.

Le temps passa et Benjamin, le petit-gros-monsieur-tranquille qui turlutait tout le temps, turlutait toujours. Les gens se bousculaient aux portes de l'opéra pour entendre le célèbre trio "turlute, tuba et harpe".

Entretemps le succès des oreillers extraordinaires diminuait de jour en jour. Les consommateurs se plaignaient.

– Vos oreillers extraordinaires sont des oreillers ordinaires!

– Vos oreillers nous empêchent de dormir!

– Vous avez endormi les gens avec votre fausse publicité! Monsieur Arthur n'y comprenait plus rien . . .

Pourquoi les oreillers n'étaient plus extraordinaires? Produisait-il trop d'oreillers à la fois ou étaient-ce les plumes qui étaient de moins bonne qualité?

Suite à tous ces malheurs monsieur Arthur tomba malade. La manufacture se trouva contrainte de fermer ses portes.

Monsieur Arthur était au lit depuis plusieurs jours et n'arrivait toujours pas à comprendre pourquoi son oreiller à lui était extraordinaire et pourquoi les nouveaux oreillers ne l'étaient pas.

– Ils ont pourtant été confectionnés de la même façon! pensait-il.

Monsieur Arthur était au bord de la crise de nerfs quand il empoigna son oreiller et mordit de toutes ses forces dedans. Tout à coup, les plumes qui y étaient enfermées s'échappèrent, laissant flotter dans la pièce le son d'une douce musique. . . C'était la voix de Benjamin et elle provenait de l'intérieur de l'oreiller.

– EURÉKA! s'écria monsieur Arthur.

Le mystère, tout comme l'oreiller, était percé.

Monsieur Arthur révéla au monde entier le secret des oreillers extraordinaires. Les gens accueillirent la nouvelle avec enthousiasme. Ils recommencèrent à acheter les oreillers de monsieur Arthur.

Monsieur Arthur supplia Benjamin de revenir travailler à la manufacture. Bien qu'il fût plutôt de nature timide et qu'il parlait peu,  Benjamin lui fit comprendre que c'était impossible car il aimait bien trop  sa nouvelle vie. Cependant, Benjamin eut une idée.

Benjamin fera une tournée internationale avec ses parents. Ainsi,
les  gens de partout pourront assister aux concerts avec leurs oreillers
qu'ils ouvriront pour que la voix de Benjamin y entre et fasse de
ces oreillers  des oreillers extraordinaires.